Search for the Squizzle!
A Lift-the-Flap Adventure

WE NEED TO TURN THE MAGIC ON,
WE NEED TO SAVE THE DAY.
COME ON!

BANTAM BOOKS

One day, Tom wanted to know how to play Squizzle, so Ariela, Twigs and Squirmtum took him to the pitch for a lesson. "This seed pod is the 'Squizzle'. You've got to throw it and hit the Wingseeds on top of those posts," said Ariela. She then threw her Squizzle, and it hit a Wingseed.

"To get the best points, you can do a Mega-Triple-Wing throw and hit all three Wingseeds in one go!" Squirmtum said.
"I want to try a Mega-Triple-Wing throw, but everyone says I'm too small . . ." sighed Twigs.
"Go on, Twigs! Give it a whirl!" Ariela cried. So Twigs got ready to throw his Squizzle.

The Squizzle flew off into
a deep, dark canyon.
"Oh no! Not down there!
I knew I was too small to
do a Mega-Triple-Wing
throw," Twigs sighed. "My
Squizzle is lost *for ever*!"
"Don't worry, Twigs," said
Tom. "I'll go down there
and get it for you."
The others gasped in horror.
"No, Tom! That's where
Rickety McGlum lives!"
"Who?" Tom wondered.
"Everyone says he's
the scariest spider in
Treetopolis," Twigs
told him.

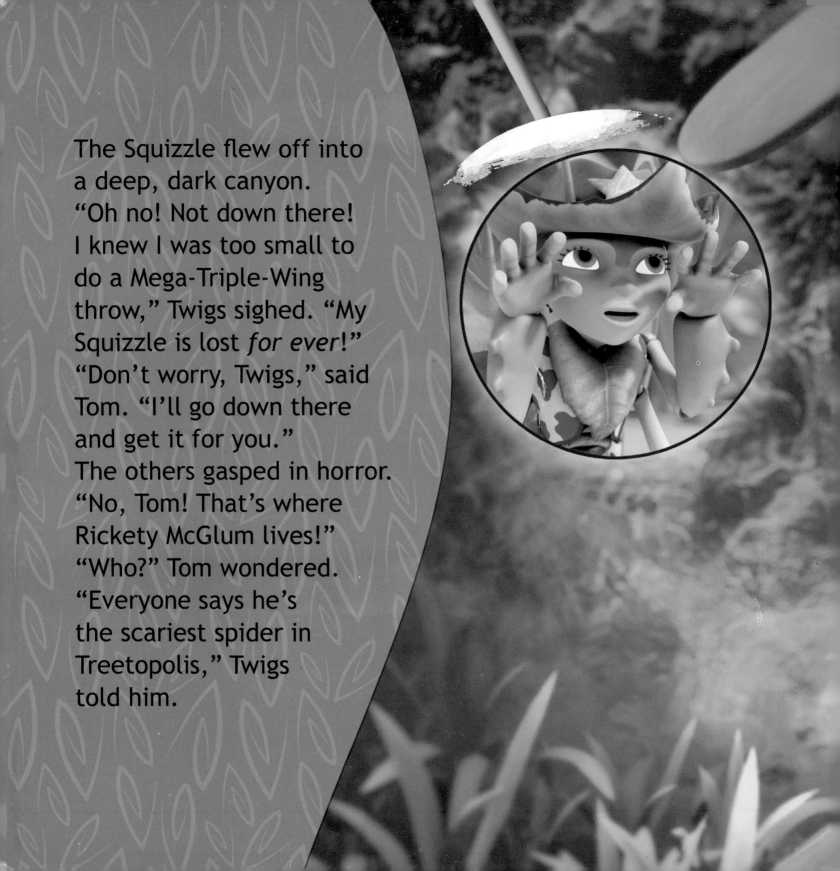

"It's OK, Twigs, I'm not scared! We'll get your Squizzle back,"
Tom said bravely, as they gazed into the canyon. "I'd feel
better if I had some magic to use, though. It's time to do the
moves to turn our magic powers on."

"Come on, join in!"

TIME FOR TREE FU!

"To make Tree Fu spells
do what you see . . .

Slide to the side,
And ***jump*** right back!
Hold your hands up high,
Spin around . . .
Reach up for the sky!"

Tom, Twigs and Ariela flew down into the canyon, and Squirmtum rolled along behind them. The grass was very tall, with cobwebs all around. "Let's be quiet, so that Rickety doesn't hear us," Ariela whispered. "Woah, that was close!" Tom yelled, as the Squizzle soared past. It was still going crazy! Tom dived to catch it, but the Squizzle was flying too fast.

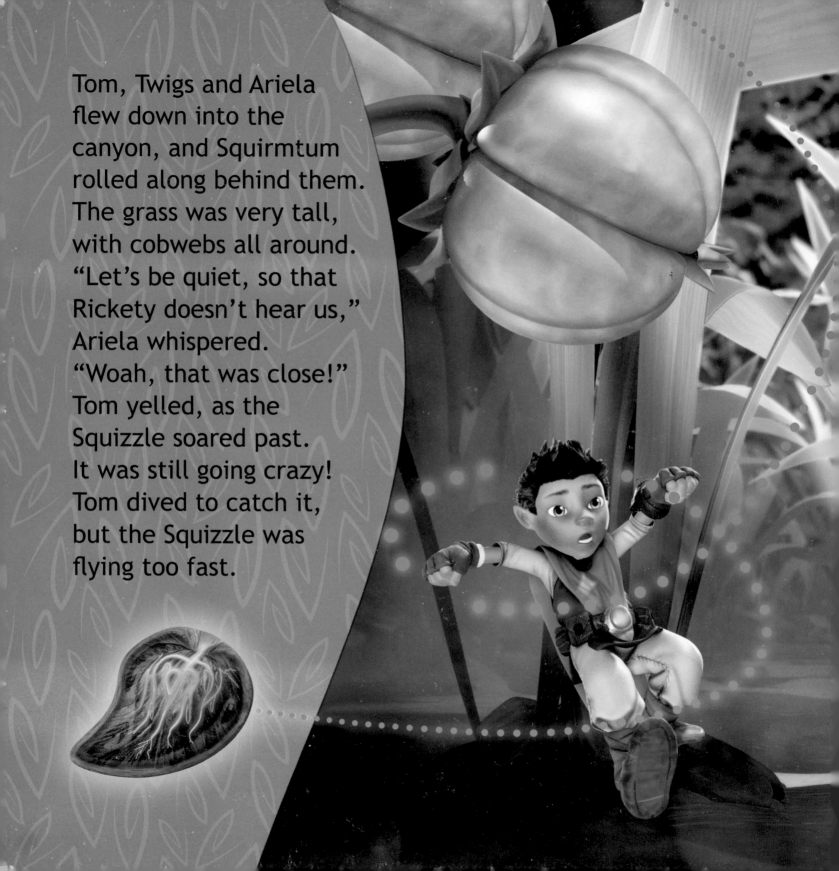

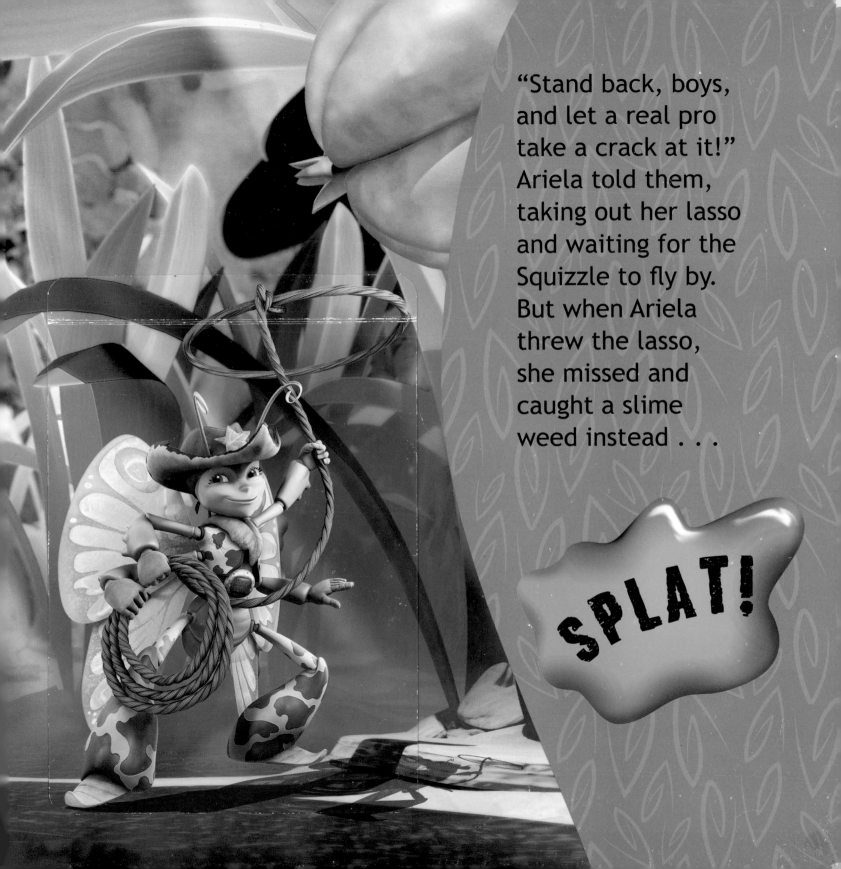

"Stand back, boys, and let a real pro take a crack at it!" Ariela told them, taking out her lasso and waiting for the Squizzle to fly by. But when Ariela threw the lasso, she missed and caught a slime weed instead . . .

SPLAT!

The slime weeds gave Tom an idea – they could use the sticky green slime to stop the Squizzle! He climbed to the top of a slime weed and took aim, but the splats kept missing. The Squizzle was moving too fast! "We need bigger splats, which means we need bigger slime weeds!" Tom decided. "It's time to do the *Grow-Grow-Grow* spell. Are you ready?"

TREE FU GO!

"Into your spell pose."

"Squat low like a frog, then grow one arm up."

"Stay low and grow the other arm up."

"Wiggle your fingers and grow them up in the middle."

"Clap and say 'Grow-Grow-Grow' to send the magic to me."

GROW- GROW- GROW!

"Are you ready, Twigs?" Tom asked.

Twigs nodded. "Let's slime that Squizzle!" he cried. They each climbed to the top of a giant slime weed and began to shoot sticky green slime at the Squizzle. But they kept missing!

"Perhaps my plan won't work, after all," Tom sighed.

WOOO!

ARRRGH!

But the celebration didn't last long, because a dark shadow with many legs appeared and began to move towards them. "It's Rickety!" The friends all gasped in panic, before hiding in the tall grass. Would he spot them? If he did, they might be stuck down in the canyon *for ever*!

Rickety, the scary spider, slowly crept closer and closer. They gasped when he raised his stick above his head.

"Oh, no!" Ariela cried, as he swung it down towards her . . .

"These slime weeds made everyone think I was scary, but it isn't true," explained Rickety.

"We should have made our minds up ourselves, instead of believing what other people said," Tom realised.

"It's the same for you, Twigs," said Rickety. "Don't listen to people who say you're too small to do a Mega-Triple-Wing throw. I can play Squizzle, so I'll teach you!"

So Twigs had got his Squizzle back, and they'd found an unexpected new friend, too!

"Thanks for helping us in Treetopolis today. See you soon for another adventure. Bye for now!"